TRIPPER'S TRAVELS
AN INTERNATIONAL SCRAPBOOK

by Nancy Kapp Chapman

illustrated by Lee Chapman

Marshall Cavendish Children

It's said, "There's a world of possibilities," and my paws itch to know them all. I'm called Tripper the Dog because I like to take trips. I am an artist, and this is my scrapbook. You'll see the places I've been and the friends I've made. I've discovered that although places, faces, and languages are different, people (and dogs) have many things in common. Kids go to school to learn about the world. Friends and families gather together to celebrate birthdays, weddings, and holidays. People are proud of their country and culture. And everywhere I go, people love their pets! (That's good for me!) Here are the ten cities that I visited. I hope you'll enjoy my scrapbook. Woof!

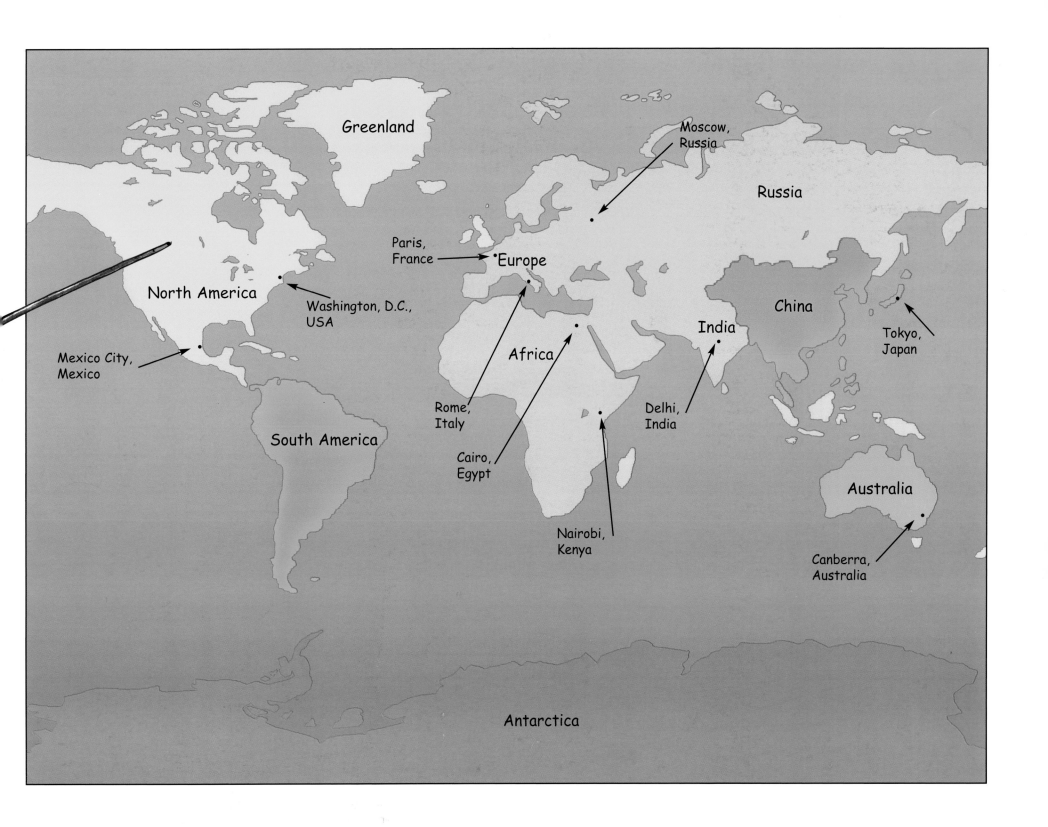

Greenland

Moscow,
Russia

Russia

Paris,
France •Europe

China

North America

Washington, D.C.,
USA

India

Tokyo,
Japan

Mexico City,
Mexico

Africa

Rome,
Italy

Delhi,
India

South America

Cairo,
Egypt

Nairobi,
Kenya

Australia

Canberra,
Australia

Antarctica

Paris, France

BONE-JOUR from PARIS

"Bone-jour," I said, when I was in Paris having my breakfast. Paris is one of the most beautiful cities in western Europe. It has great monuments, such as the Eiffel Tower and the Arc de Triomphe, and incredible museums and cathedrals. Best of all, I could sit in a sidewalk café and watch the world go by. The nice thing about Paris—people can bring their dogs to restaurants!

My friend, Pablo Pigasso, and I in front of the Centre Georges Pompidou.

This museum is really something! It's like a building turned inside out. On the outside, you can see its pipes and vents in different colors. Blue is for air conditioning, green for water, yellow for electricity, red for heat, and so on.

Paris is the capital of France.

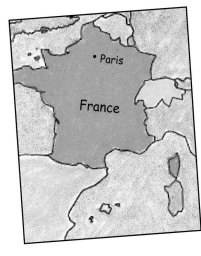

Drifting down the Seine with Notre Dame in the background

You can take a boat trip on the Seine River. It runs through the heart of Paris. I rented a doggy houseboat.

Me with a gargoyle

The Eiffel Tower is the symbol of Paris. It has two and a half million rivets holding it together! It blew me away!

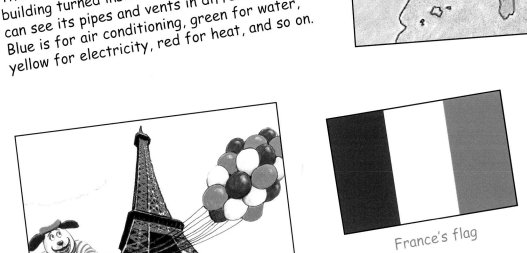

France's flag

Stamp

The gargoyles at the top of Notre Dame Cathedral have a great view. They were carved to look scary to protect the building. Some of them are water-spouts. Ha-ha. They "gargoyle" water.

French
chapeau

French
béret

French
toque

This is a French chef's hat. It has 100 pleats because a French chef knows 100 ways to cook eggs!

Paris is filled with great cooking. I tried some new dishes: *escargots* (snails), *pâté* (goose liver), and *cuisses de grenouilles* (frogs' legs). Paris has world-famous cooking schools. Fifi took me to the Bone Appétit Institute, where I learned to make *crème brûlée*.

Parisian clothing is *très chic*. It's called *haute couture* which means "high style." I'm at the Louis Vui-bone show where there are designer clothes even for dogs. I'm sitting with my friend, Fifi, a French poodle who works for *Dogue Magazine*.

French pastries

Bastille Day

French fire truck

Arc de Triomphe

Here are some French words that I learned:
hello—bonjour
good-bye—au revoir
good morning—bonjour
good evening—bonsoir
good night—bonne nuit
please—s'il vous plaît
thank you—merci
you're welcome—de rien
excuse me—excusez-moi
how are you?—comment allez-vous?
well, thank you —bien, merci

July 14th is Bastille Day, France's Independence Day. It's filled with celebrations, parades, and fireworks. Jets fly over the Champs-Élysées blowing out red, white, and blue smoke. French firemen, called *Pompiers de Paris*, hold parties at the stations. I'm up on a fire-station roof with Fifi and a pack of friends.

I waved *au revoir* and shed a big tear. "Good-bye, dear friends, see you next year."

Rome, Italy

Look at me at the opera, shouting "BRAVA" to a famous soprano. I love the city of Rome. It has many ancient buildings, cathedrals, and fountains. It's filled with statues, paintings, and murals by great artists such as Leonardo da Vinci and Michelangelo. The Italians have great food, too—lots of pasta and pizza. Not good for my waistline!

I am Guido from Milano,
A speedy Greyhound Italiano!
For the price of a bone,
I'll show you Rome.

There's a saying that goes, "All roads lead to Rome." I'm standing at the Appian Way which was built thousands of years ago. I'm with my friend, Guido, who showed me around the city.

Italy's flag

Rome is the capital of Italy.

Here we are on a street called Via Veneto. We went shopping for clothes and shoes by famous designers—Armani, Gucci, and my favorite—PUCCI!

This is the beautiful Basilica of St. Peter in Vatican City, where the pope lives.

Here is the Pantheon—maybe the first building ever built with a freestanding dome.

Pizza was originally eaten by farmers until a baker in Naples made a special pizza for Queen Margherita of Italy in 1889. It was a BIG HIT.

Pizza margherita

Ziti

Manicotti

Macaroni

Rigatoni

Spaghetti

Lasagne

Fettucini

Penne

Fusilli

I'm in the *piazza* (square) by the Spanish Steps. They lead to a church called the Trinità dei Monte. *Piazzas* are the center of life in Rome. People fill the cafés, and children dance to the music of strolling musicians. I'm eating *gelato*, Italian ice cream. Yum!

Espresso machine

Different flavors of gelato

I'm sitting at a café, eating again. See the cat in the background? He was just waiting for me to drop some food. Rome is home to hundreds of stray cats.

Gladiators marching in front of the Colosseum

Roman cat

Here are some Italian words that I learned:
hello, good morning—buon giorno
good-bye—arrivedérci
good evening—buona sera
good night—buona notte
thank you—grazie
you're welcome—prego
please—per favore
excuse me—mi scusi
how are you?—come sta?
good—bene
so-so—cosi, cosi

Happy birthday to Rome! There's a legend that Rome was founded on April 21, 753 B.C. That's why on April 21, Romans dress up as gladiators and hold a special celebration. They march to the Colosseum, where they fought lions and tigers—big cats!—in the old days. See you later, gladiator.

The Trevi Fountain

Stamp

Gladiator's sword

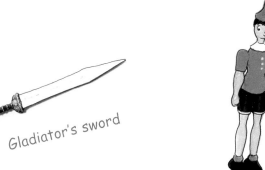

A wooden Pinocchio toy—Pinocchio was a puppet who wanted to be a real boy in a story by Carlo Collodi.

"Throw a coin in the fountain," so they say,
"And you'll come back to Rome someday."
So it is, with a smile and a sigh,
I say, "Adiós, arrivedérci, good-bye."

Cairo, Egypt

I'm outside of Cairo riding Samel the Camel after a rare rainstorm. You can see the pyramids and the Great Sphinx of Giza in the background. The pyramids were built by the *pharaohs*, the kings of ancient Egypt. See my friend Shani sitting next to those Egyptians? She's a pharaoh hound, one of the oldest dog breeds in the world. To me, she acts just like a puppy.

Look at me with my binoculars and mint tea! I'm standing on a rooftop, and you can see an ancient mosque and minaret in the background.

Egypt's flag

The ancient Egyptians put dog and cat mummies in their tombs so their pets could join them in the next world. I hope I don't end up a mummy!

Cairo is the capital of Egypt. It is the largest city in Africa and is VERY OLD.

Hieroglyphics

The Egyptians wrote in pictures called hieroglyphs. They also invented a paper which they called papyrus.

Here I'm taking a picture of the minarets of the Al-Azhar Mosque. This beautiful mosque is also a famous university.

The Khan Al-Khalili Bazaar

We dressed in *galabayas*—long robes of cotton material. They are great to wear in hot weather. I wore a turban and Shani wore a scarf. Egyptians also dress as we do in the States, but they don't like to show too much skin. You rarely see them in shorts or sleeveless shirts.

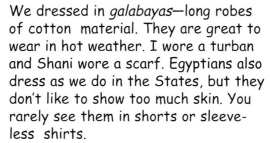

Lamb kebabs

In the center of Cairo is an old market known as the *khan*. Shani and I wandered around the narrow alleys and poked our noses into shops that sold lots of great stuff, even dog collars.

All the seeing and sniffing made me hungry. Here's what we ate for lunch: pita bread, *kufta* (meatballs), *molokhiyya* soup, *baba ghanoush* (eggplant), *hummus* (chickpea mixture), *kebabs* (lamb and veggies on a skewer), *ruz* (rice), *batatis* (potatoes), lentils, and yogurt. For dessert I had *baklava* (pastry with honey and nuts) along with dates, melons, and nuts. Sure beats dog chow!

This is the street of spices. What a treat for our doggy noses. We sniffed anise, chamomile, hibiscus, cinnamon, and chiles. The chiles made me sneeze!

Baklava

Scarab beetle

Travel poster

Spice market

Shani took me to an Egyptian wedding where everyone is welcome—even a dog like me. The bride and groom are greeted by *a zaffa*, a procession of musicians, singers, and dancers. The *Tanura* dancers whirl around for thirty minutes, sometimes more. I just had to try it, and woof!, did I get dizzy.

Sunset on the Nile

Dumbek

Tambourine

Oud

Stamp

In a graceful *felluca*, we sailed down the Nile. "*Laila tiaba* and good night," I said with a smile.

NAIROBI, KENYA

Here I am with some animals in Nairobi National Park, just a few miles from downtown Nairobi. I bet those people working in those tall buildings can look down and see the animals!

Kenya's flag

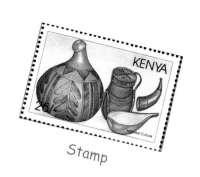

Stamp

Aren't I lucky? I'm getting a hug from a baby elephant. He lives at the Daphne Sheldrick Elephant Orphanage, where people care for baby elephants and rhinos who have lost their mothers. When the animals are ready, they get released back into the wild.

I stayed in a hotel called Giraffe Manor. It's about eight miles from Nairobi. Look at me feeding the giraffes from my second-floor-bedroom window!

Nairobi is the capital of Kenya in Africa and has dozens of national parks and wildlife reserves.

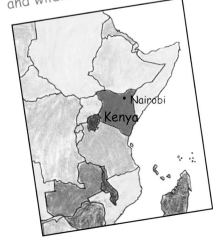

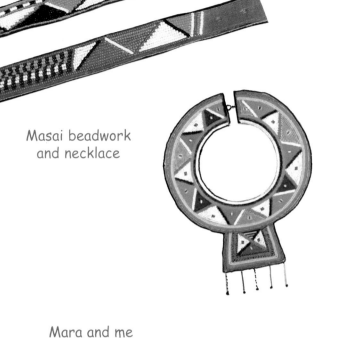

Masai beadwork
and necklace

Mara and me

I'm standing next to my friend, Mara, a member of the
Masai tribe. Mara sells beaded jewelry at the market.
The colors, shapes, and patterns of the necklaces tell a
woman's age, if she's married, and how many children
she has. Nicer than a dog collar!

See all the fruit and vegetables in the Nairobi City Market? Mara is buying food
for our lunch.

ugali

Kenya's national dish is *ugali*, a porridge
made with cornmeal. You eat it with
your hands (or paws) along with *nyama
choma*—barbecued goat meat.

Masai Jumping Dance

The Masai celebrate important events with songs and dances. They have a dance in which they leap high in the air. It's an honor to be the highest jumper. When I jumped, I fell on my tail. So embarrassing!

West African Djembe drum

The Masai and most Kenyans speak Swahili (Kiswahili). Here are some words I learned:

hello—jambo
good-bye—kwa heri
good morning—habari za asubuhi
good afternoon—habarai za mchana
good night—habara za usiku
please—tafad hali
thank you—asante
excuse me—hebu
how are you?—habarai?
(I am) fine—sijambo

On the road to Kilimanjaro

"Kwa heri," I said as I waved good-bye. "Asante for my day with the Masai!"

Moscow, Russia

Here I am, chugging into the Moscow train station. I rode the famous Trans-Siberian Railway.
My Russian friends, the Borzois, greeted me.

I'm in Red Square, the center of Moscow. I'm looking for information about Russian dogs. Behind me you can see the State History Museum.

Moscow is the capital of Russia, the largest country in the world when I visited.

Travel brochure

Olga lives with her brothers, Sasha and Ivan. From the window, we can see St. Basil's Cathedral. We are drinking Russian tea made in a samovar.

It can get very cold in Moscow, so I'm shopping for some warm clothes with my friend Olga. We went to the GUM department store. It takes up one whole side of Red Square. I bought mittens for my front paws.

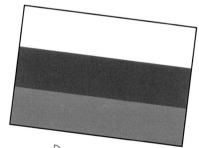

Russia's flag

Russian souvenir sign

A stamp with a samovar

I went to see Olga dance in the Borzoi Ballet. It made my day!

The Russians love to eat. Yum, yum. Here are some of the foods I tried: *pirozhki* (meat pastries), *kulebiaka* (salmon or cabbage rolls), *golubtsy* (stuffed cabbage), *borscht* (beet soup), *beef stroganoff* (beef with mushrooms and sour cream), *blinis* (buckwheat pancakes), and *caviar* (fish eggs). Also, lots of potatoes and black bread. For dessert I had *morozhenoe* (ice cream)!

Stamp

Then we heard some folksingers play,

Russian McDonald's sign

and we rode in a real Russian sleigh.

Matrioshka dolls
("little mothers")—
one goes inside another.

I learned to speak some Russian:
hello—zdravstuyte
good-bye—do-svidaniya
good morning—dobroe utro
good afternoon—dobry den
good night—dobry vyecher
thank you—spasibo
you're welcome—pashaluista
please—pazhaluysta
excuse me—prasteete
how are you?—kak pazhivayesh?
I'm okay—neepolaha

Maslyanitsa is a carnival at the beginning of Lent that celebrates the coming of spring. People dress up in costumes and burn a scarecrow. Everyone eats *blinis* (pancakes) which are round like the sun. *Blinis* are served with honey, caviar, cream, and butter. I tried not to drool on my costume.

Blinis

And with a great Russian bear hug, I was on my way. "*Do-svidaniya* and good-bye, I'll come back someday!"

Delhi, India

This is the Chandni Chowk, the market in the middle of Old Delhi. You can buy anything there, from a washing machine to a wedding dress. Maybe even an elephant! So much is going on all the time. What sights! What smells! I was shopping for Indian Dog-Chowk.

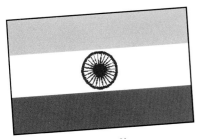

India's flag

Flying high over the Taj

Whee! I'm flying over the Taj Mahal in a hot-air balloon! The Taj is about 200 miles from Delhi. It took 20,000 workers and more than 22 years to build! It made me want to howl!

Red Fort (Lal Qila)

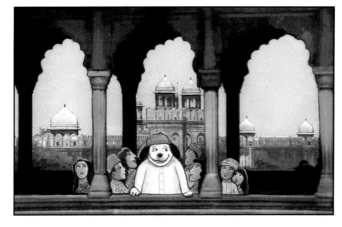

I'm standing with some tourists at the Red Fort (Lal Qila). There are lawns, plazas, gardens, and pools behind its red walls.

Stamp

The Qatab Minar is the tallest stone tower in India.

Rupee (Indian money)

Delhi is the capital of India. It has two sections—Old Delhi and New Delhi. Old Delhi is filled with bazaars and palaces. New Delhi is more modern, with big buildings and wide streets.

Zipping past the Indian Gate in a three-wheel motor rickshaw

This is the India Gate. It was built to honor the soldiers who died in World War I and two other wars.

Feasting like a mogul

> I am Devi, dog of New Delhi. I play my sitar on the Indian tellie.

India makes more movies than any other country. Every year, New Delhi has an international film festival. "Say chow, now!"

A woman wears a *bindi* on her forehead between the eyebrows. It might be a simple red dot or a glimmering stone.

Tandoor oven

My friend Devi and I are eating an Indian meal cooked in a *tandoor* oven, India's version of a barbecue. Meats and fish are cooked on skewers, and bread (*naan*) is cooked on the sides of the oven. I had *daal* (lentil soup), *tandoori* shrimp, and *basmati* rice with chicken *tikka*. The chicken was marinated in yogurt and lime juice with lots of spices. It was dog-licious!

Some Indians decorate their hands and feet with designs painted with henna. They call this process *mehndi*. I don't think my paws could take it.

This woman is wearing a *sari*— a wide piece of cloth wrapped around the waist and then draped over the shoulder or head.

A man wears a *kurta*, a loose-fitting shirt. Look at me! I'm wearing a cotton one. I'm also wearing an ornamental hat, like a lot of men in India. They wear turbans, too.

The Indians speak fourteen main languages. One village sometimes can't understand the language in another village a few miles away. Most people speak *Hindi*. Here are some of the words I learned:

hello, good-bye, good afternoon, good evening—namaste
good morning—subh prabhaat
good night—subh raatri
please—kripya
thank you—danyavaad
excuse me—sharmma kare
how are you?—aap kaise hain?
good—acca

Diwali is the beautiful festival of lights at the start of the Hindu New Year. It lasts for five days. People visit friends and family, taking gifts of sweets and candy. Many people make *rangoli*, a design of colored sand or powder outside their houses. *Diyas* or oil lamps are lit in the houses and shops and carried through the streets. Around 9:00 P.M., the fireworks start, and the whole of India is lit up.

"*Namaste*," I said, going away.
It has many meanings—a good thing to say.
"Hello, good-bye, and have a good day.
I'll be back to visit again and play."

Tokyo, Japan

(BOW-WA-KONICHI-WA FROM JAPAN)

Here I am in Tokyo's Ueno Park. I went to see the cherry blossoms that bloom in April. There is a pretty shrine in the park, and in the distance you can see the Imperial Palace, where the emperor lives. I'm bowing to my friends the Akita sisters. Bow-wow-wow.

This is the beautiful Sensoji temple in Asakusa, one of the oldest neighborhoods in Tokyo. These children have come to visit. The girls are dressed in traditional *kimonos*, and the boys are wearing *haori* jackets. When they go home they will probably put on jeans and T-shirts.

This is my friend Inu. He lives in Tokyo's Ginza district. Inu invited me to a tea ceremony. I brought him a gift, an American dog biscuit. When entering a Japanese house, you take off your shoes and sit on the floor—which is nice for us dogs!

Kimono

Japan's flag

Look at me! I'm taking a bath in the Sela-Onsen hot springs outside the city. That's Mount Fuji in the background. I'm doing the doggy paddle.

Japan is a bunch of islands off the east coast of Asia. Its capital is Tokyo, on the island of Honshu.

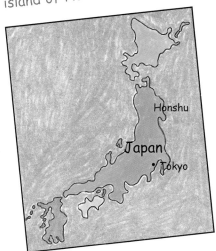

Honshu

Japan

Tokyo

Chopsticks

Inu took me to see the famous Tsukiji fish market. The Japanese love fish. Their favorites are *sushi* (raw fish with rice) and *sashimi* (raw fish). They eat both with soy sauce, ginger, and *wasabi* (horseradish).

Later we ate at a *sushi* bar near the market. I had trouble using the chopsticks. Hard to use with paws!

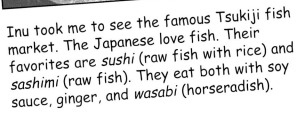

ginger · maki (roll) · anago (eel) · maguro (tuna) · ika (squid)

wasabi (horseradish)

special roll · ikura (salmon eggs) · hamachi (yellowtail) · ebi (shrimp)

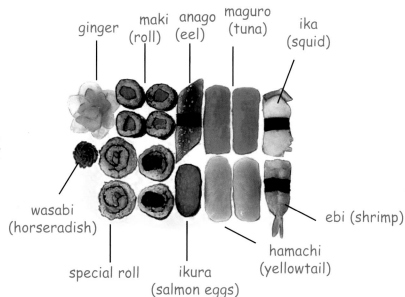

Cherry blossoms

Manekineko (Japanese cat), which brings good luck

Hagoita—a paddle for
a game like badminton

Japanese (*Nihongo*) mainly is spoken in
Japan. Here are some words I learned:
hello, good afternoon—kon-nichiwa
good-bye—sayonara
good morning—ohayo gozaimasu
good night—oyasumi nasai
please—douzo
thank you—arigato
you're welcome—do itashimashite
excuse me—sumimasen
how are you?—ogenki desu ka?
well, thank you—hai, geni desu

On Children's Day, the sky is filled with carp kites. Inside,
there are displays of *samurai* warrior dolls. Only boys used to
celebrate this holiday, but now girls do, too. I don't think
there is a celebration for dogs—yet!

Stamp

Samurai warrior

"Sayonara, good-bye. Thank you for the day."
"Oyasumi nasai, good night. Please come again
and play."

CANBERRA, AUSTRALIA

Here's a picture of me at the National Zoo and Aquarium. I made some unusual friends (from left to right): Kiki the Kangaroo, Pete the Platypus, Ringo the Dingo, (that's me in the middle), Ernie the Emu, Billy the Bandicoot, Willy the Wombat, Clyde the Koala, and Wally the Wallaby. Oh, and Kookie the Kookaburra is in a tree somewhere. Can you find her?

Government House in Canberra

Canberra is the capital of Australia. Sometimes Australia is called "down under" because it's near the bottom of the world.

Canberra was chosen as the capital of Australia in 1913. This is where the governor-general lives. Ringo and I thought we might see him.

Surf's up at Bondi Beach!

Since Sydney is just a hop, skip, and splash from Canberra, I decided to get wet. Here I am surfing the famous Bondi Beach. Hot doggy!

Australia's flag

Stamp

Look at me! I'm parasailing over Sydney Harbor. You can see the world-famous Opera House below. (I flew so high that I started singing soprano!)

Here are some Aborigine inventions:

Boomerang: invented for hunting, it comes back to you when you throw it.

Didgeridoo: a musical instrument like a trumpet.

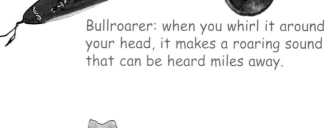

Bullroarer: when you whirl it around your head, it makes a roaring sound that can be heard miles away.

Here I am in the lobby of the National Museum of Australia in Canberra. What an incredible building! It looks like a giant jigsaw puzzle. The museum has exhibits of Australia's past, present, and future. My favorite was the gallery of Australia's first people, the Aborigines.

Road sign

How do I look in my *Akubra* hat and *Driza-bone* long oilskin coat? You can see clothes like this in the "outback" or countryside of Australia.

DANGER CROCODILES NO SWIMMING

Pavlova (served with fruit and cream)

Lamingtons

Vegemite

On my last day, Ringo the Dingo and I were invited to a barbecue. We ate *chook* (chicken), *yabbies* (crayfish), *damper* (bread), and *Vegemite* sandwiches. *Vegemite* is a spread made from yeast, veggies, and spices. For dessert, we ate *pavlova* (a meringue cake) and *lamingtons* (sponge cake dipped in chocolate and coconut). Drool-icious!

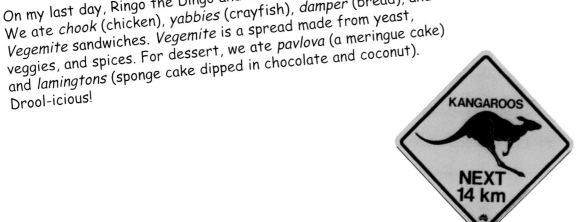

KANGAROOS
NEXT
14 km

Road sign

"So long, my friends . . . it's been a true wonder.
I'll be back again soon to see you 'down under.'"

Mexico City, Mexico

Here I am in Plaza Garibaldi where the *mariachis* (Mexican musicians) come to play. They play guitars, violins, and trumpets, and all of the musicians know how to sing. My favorite song is "La Cucaracha."

I am standing in the Zócalo, the grand plaza in the city's center. You can see the Metropolitan Cathedral in the background. I'm buying cotton candy from my friend, Senor Chihuahua.

Mexico's flag

Mexico's capital is Mexico City, the largest Spanish-speaking city in the world.

Mexico

• Mexico City

Stamp

This pyramid is located in Teotihuacan (tee-oh-tee-wack-an) north of Mexico City. It was built by the Aztecs, the original people of Mexico.

Here I am in Xochimilco (so-chee-mil-co), Mexico City's floating gardens. Colorful boats cruise these canals with parties of Mexican families—especially on Sundays. I've just bought some flowers from a floating flower seller.

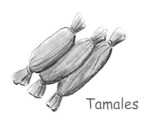

Tamales

Tacos

Chiles

Sombrero

Serape

Huaraches

Rebozo

Huipil

Tortillas

I'm eating lunch with my friend Carmen. Great *guacamole!* The Mexicans use a lot of *chiles* (spicy!) and *tortillas* in their cooking. They add corn and beans to many of their dishes (which sometimes gives me gas). I like their *enchiladas, tacos,* and *quesadillas.* And their *tamales* are great, too. They make them with cornmeal.

Travel brochure

In the *mercado,* I bought a big *sombrero* (hat), a colorful *serape* (blanket), and some *huaraches* (sandals) for my paws. The women wear *rebozos* (scarves) and beautiful *huipils* (dresses).

Many Mexicans take a *siesta* after lunch. Then they go back to work. Nice custom!

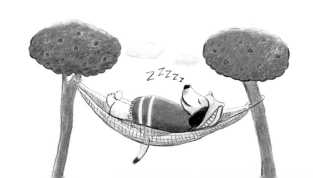

Carmen invited me to her birthday *fiesta*. We played fun games and ate good food. The *mariachis* sang "Las Mañanitas," the Mexican birthday song. The best part was hanging up a *piñata*. It was filled with candy and toys. We took turns trying to break it open. Carmen's friends blindfolded me and spun me around until I was dizzy. I broke it! Carmen said that meant I'd have good luck.

Piñata

Here are some Spanish words that I learned:
hello—hola
good-bye—adiós
good morning—buenos días
good afternoon—buenas tardes
good night—buenas noches
thank you—gracias
you're welcome—de nada
excuse me—perdón
how are you?—¿cómo está?
well, thank you—bien, gracias
what's your name?—¿cómo se llama?

Adiós.

Buenas noches.

"*Adiós*" (good-bye) and "*buenas noches*" (good night).
Gracias for the *fiesta*—it was a delight.

Here I am, back in the U.S.A. I'm standing on the steps of the Capitol building with some other dogs. Pete the Pit Bull got a permit from the police department to demonstrate for Paw Power!

Washington, D.C. (District of Columbia) is the capital of the United States.

United States of America

Senate seal

Congressional seal

Library of Congress

Here I am in the Library of Congress. It has information on every country in the world. I am researching dogs of the world. Arf!

Union Station

Union Station used to be the largest train station in the world. Today it has a shopping mall, restaurants, and a movie theater. Crab cakes are a D.C. specialty, but I settled for a hot dog.

This is the Washington Monument, built to honor George Washington, the first president of the United States. I believe it is the tallest stone structure in the world!

American flag

Owney's tags and badges

National Postal Museum

Owney was a homeless dog that the Albany postal clerks adopted in 1888. He loved the smell of mailbags. He traveled on trains across the U.S., protecting the mail. He even traveled to Asia and Europe. When he returned, he had so many tags and badges on his collar that John Wanamaker, the postmaster general, gave him a special vest to display them. Now, he's a dog I would like to have known.

"The Castle," the information center at the Smithsonian Museum

The Smithsonian has fifteen different museums. It would take many days to see all of them. Pete and I visited the National Postal Museum and the National Museum of Natural History.

Franklin D. Roosevelt Memorial

This is the memorial to Franklin Delano Roosevelt, the thirty-second president of the United States. I patted the statue of Fala, his Scottish terrier. The president took him on many trips. Fala met lots of famous people and entertained them with his tricks. At breakfast, Fala was served a bone while the president ate his own breakfast. Fala got tons of fan mail. Lucky Fala!

National Museum of Natural History

SABER-TOOTH TIGER (C.SNAPUS)

At the National Museum of Natural History, we saw the skeletons and fossils of huge dinosaurs. Some of them were millions of years old. Talk about old bones!

In front of the White House

Stamp

License plate

Since I'm a dog, I managed to sneak by security onto the grounds of the White House. I sat on the lawn and took off my hat—and got a surprise presidential pat!

This is a drawing I made of me with Lots of the Friends I met.

Mara the African Wild Dog

Inu the Japanese Akita

Devi the mutt from India

Carmen the Mexican Chihuahua

Me

Guido the Italian Greyhound

Shani the Egyptian Pharaoh Hound

Ringo the Australian Dingo

Fifi the French Poodle

Olga the Russian Borzoi

Pete the American Pit Bull

I've taken some wonderful trips, but there are still many other countries I want to visit. I can go to the library, find stuff on the Internet, and read stories about other places . . . but I think the world would be better if we could ALL visit at least one foreign city and make friends with people (and dogs) from a different culture. We should look for the things we share rather than the things that separate us. The journey never ends if along the way we make friends!

This is sort of how some foreign words sound:

French

hello/good morning—bonjour (bohn-zhoor)
good-bye—au revoir (oh) (reh-vwah)
good evening—bonsoir (bohn-swahr)
good night—bonne nuit (bun) (nwee)
please—s'il vous plaît (seel) (voo) (play)
thank you—merci (mair-see)
you're welcome—de rien (duh) (ree-yen)
excuse me—excusez-moi (ek-skew-zay-mwah)
how are you?—comment allez-vous? (koh-mahn)
    (tah-lay-voo)
well, thank you—bien, merci (bee-yen) (mair-see)

Italian

hello/good morning—buon giorno (boo-ohn) (jor-no)
good-bye—arrivedérci (ah-ree-veh-der-chee)
good evening—buona sera (boo-ohn-ah) (seh-rah)
good night—buona notte (boo-ohn-ah) (noht-teh)
thank you—grazie (grah-tsee-eh)
you're welcome—prego (pray-goh)
please—per favore (pehr) (fah-voh-reh)
excuse me—mi scusi (mee) (skuzi)
how are you?—come sta? (koh-meh) (stah)
good—bene (beh-neh)
so-so—cosi, cosi (koh-see) (koh-see)

Arabic

hello—ahlan wa sahlan (ah-lan) (wa) (sah-lan)
good-bye—ma'a salaema (ma) (salamah)
good morning—saba'a il-kheer (sabah) (el-kair)
good afternoon—mas'a il-kheer (masa) (el-kair)
thank you—shukran (shoo-kran)
you're welcome—afwan (ef-won)
please—min fadlak (min) (fodh-lock)
excuse me—assif (os-eef)
how are you?—kaifa halok? (keef) (halek)
very well—tamam (ta-mom)

Swahili

hello—jambo (jam-boh)
good-bye—kwa heri (kwah) (heri)
good morning—habari za asubuhi (hub-ari) (za)
    (os-oo-boo-hee)
good afternoon—habarai za mchana (hub-arai) (za)
    (moo-chana)
good night—habara za usiku (hub-ara) (za) (oos-ee-koo)
please—tafad hali (taf-odd) (ali)
thank you—asante (ah-san-tay)
excuse me—hebu (hey-boo)
how are you?—habarai? (hub-ar-ai)
(I am) fine—sijambo (see-jam-boh)

Russian

hello—zdravstuyte (zdrah-st-vooy-teh)
good-bye—do-svidaniya (da-svee-da-nee-ya)
good morning—dobroe utro (dob-raye) (ootro)
good afternoon—dobry den (dob-ree) (den)
good night—dobry vyecher (dob-ree) (vye-cher)
thank you—spasibo (spa-see-bo)
you're welcome—pashaluista (pa-zha-looy-sta)
please—pazhaluysta (pa-zha-loo-sta)
excuse me—prasteete (pra-stee-te)
how are you?—kak pazhivayesh? (kak) (pazhi-vayesh)
I'm okay—neepolaha (nee-ploh-ha)

Hindi

hello, good-bye, good afternoon, good evening—namaste
  (na-may-stay)
good morning—subh prabhaat (shubh) (prob-hot)
good night—subh raatri (shubh) (raa-thri)
please—kripya (krip-ya)
thank you—danyavaad (dhan-ya-vad)
excuse me—sharmma kare (kshamma) (kar-ren)
how are you?—ap kaise hain? (ap) (kay-sey) (heh)
Good—acca (a-chaa)

Japanese

hello, good afternoon—kon-nichiwa (kohn-nee-chee-wah)
good-bye—sayonara (sah-yoh-nah-rah)
good morning—ohayo gozaimasu (oh-hah-yoh)
  (goh-zye-mahss)
good night—oyasumi nasai (oh-yah-soo-mee) (nahj-sigh)
please—douzo (doo-zoh)
thank you—arigato (ah-ree-gah-toh)
you're welcome—do itashimashite (doh)
  (eee-tah-shee-mahsh-the)
excuse me—sumimasen (see-mee-mah-sen)
how are you?—ogenki desu ka? (oh-gen-kee) (dess) (kah)
well, thank you—hai, geni desu (hi) (gen-kee) (dess)

Spanish

hello—hola (oh-lah)
good-bye—adiós (ah-dee-ohs)
good morning—buenos días (bweh-nohs) (dee-ahs)
good afternoon—buenas tardes (bweh-nahs) (tar-deys)
good night—buenas noches (bweh-nahs) (noh-cheys)
thank you—gracias (grah-see-ahs)
you're welcome—de nada (deh) (nah-dah)
excuse me—perdón (pair-dohn)
how are you?—¿cómo está? (koh-moh) (es-tah)
well, thank you—bien, gracias (bee-en) (grah-see-ahs)
what's your name?—¿cómo se llama? (coh-moh) (seh)
  (yah-mah)

To my sister, Laura Kapp, who has devoted her career in
E.S.L. education to the children of the world
—N.K.C.

To Margery and Anahid, for their help in bringing Tripper to the world
—L.C.

Text copyright © 2005 by Nancy Kapp Chapman
Illustrations copyright © 2005 by Lee Chapman
All rights reserved
Marshall Cavendish, 99 White Plains Road, Tarrytown, NY 10591
www.marshallcavendish.us
Library of Congress Cataloging-in-Publication Data
Chapman, Nancy Kapp.
Tripper's travels : an international scrapbook / by Nancy Kapp Chapman ; illustrated by Lee Chapman.— 1st ed.
p. cm.
Summary: Tripper the Dog keeps a scrapbook detailing his travel to big cities all around the world.
ISBN 0-7614-5240-0
[1. Travel—Fiction. 2. Scrapbooks—Fiction. 3. Dogs—Fiction.] I. Chapman, Lee, ill. II. Title.

PZ7.C3722Tr 2005
[E]—dc22
2004027457
ISBN: 0-7614-5240-0

The Russian McDonald's logo is used with permission from McDonald's Corporation

The text of this book is set in Comic Sans.
The illustrations are rendered using oil paint, oil pastel, prismacolor pencil, and Photoshop.

Printed in China
First edition
1 3 5 6 4 2